W9-BNS-544

double-cross

By Eleanor Robins

SADDLEBACK
EDUCATIONAL PUBLISHING

C H O I C E S

Break All Rules

Broken Promise

Don't Get Caught

Double-Cross

Easy Pass

Friend or Foe?

No Exceptions

No Limits

Pay Back

Trust Me

SADDLEBACK
EDUCATIONAL PUBLISHING
www.sdlback.com

ISBN-13: 978-1-61651-595-9
ISBN-10: 1-61651-595-3
eBook: 978-1-61247-241-6

Printed in Guangzhou, China
0411/04-25-11

15 14 13 12 11   1 2 3 4 5

Meet the Characters from

double-cross

Braden: desperately wants a used car he sees in an ad but doesn't have any money

Braden's Dad: encourages Braden to get a job and save up for a car purchase

Kwame: looking for a summer job, one of Braden's friends from school

Mr. Duvall: owner of the local hardware store

chapter 1

Braden was at home. He was out of school for the summer. And it was the first morning he didn't have to go to school.

He went into the kitchen. It was almost time for breakfast.

His mom said, "Breakfast isn't ready yet, Braden."

"Do I have time to read the paper before we eat?" Braden asked.

"You can read it for a few minutes. But not for long," his mom said.

Braden wanted to read the car ads. So he hurried into the den. He knew the paper would be in there.

His dad was in the den. He was reading the paper.

"Can I read some of the paper, Dad?" Braden asked.

"Sure, Braden. Which part do you want?" his dad asked.

"The used car ads," Braden said.

His dad gave him that part of the paper. Braden said, "Thanks, Dad."

Braden started to read the ads about used cars for sale. His dad read the other part of the paper. The two read for a few minutes.

Then his dad put the other part of the paper on a table. And he went into the kitchen.

Braden read five or six more ads. Then he found just the car he wanted.

And it was the right price for him. He could hardly wait to tell his dad and mom about the car.

His mom called to him from the kitchen. She said, "Breakfast is ready, Braden."

"Okay, Mom. Thanks," Braden said. Braden put the paper down on the table. And he went into the kitchen. His mom and dad were at the kitchen table.

Braden quickly sat down at the table. He put some food on his plate. Then he started to eat his breakfast. He ate for a few minutes.

Then he said, "I saw an ad in the paper. A car dealer has a used car for sale. And it sounds just like what I want. And it's the right price for me."

His mom said, "What kind of car is it, Braden? And how much does it cost?" Braden told his mom.

His dad said, "It doesn't matter what kind of car it is. Or how much it costs. Braden doesn't have any money to buy a car."

"You could loan me the money, Dad. And I could pay you back," Braden said. "With what, Braden? You don't have any money," his dad said.

"I can get a job. And I can make some money. Will you loan me the money for the car? And let me pay you back later?" Braden asked.

"I'll be glad to help you get a car, Braden. But I won't make it easy for you. First, you'll have to earn some money. So you'd better get busy and find a job," his dad said.

"But where?" Braden asked.

"I don't know, Braden. You'll have to look for one. And you should start doing that today. Or the summer will be gone before you know it. And you still won't have a job," his dad said.

"What about the car I read about in the ad?" Braden asked.

"What about it?" his dad said.

"Can I call about it?" Braden asked.

His dad said, "You can call about it, Braden. But it would be a waste of your time. You can't buy it."

Braden thought his dad would say that. But Braden still had to ask him.

"Make some money this summer, Braden. And then look for a car," his dad said.

Braden knew what he had to do. He had to look for a job. And he had to do it quickly. Before some other teens got all of the summer jobs.

chapter

2

It was the same morning. Breakfast was over. And Braden's dad was ready to go to work.

His dad told his mom good-bye. Then his dad looked over at Braden. He said, "A lot of kids might be looking for summer jobs. So you'd better get busy and look for a job today, Braden. Or all of the summer jobs might be gone."

"Okay, Dad. I'll look for one today," Braden said.

But where should he look first?

His dad had to go to work. So Braden didn't have time to ask him. Braden's dad left to go to work.

Braden looked over at his mom. He said, "That used car is just what I want, Mom. Can you get Dad to loan me the money for the car?"

His mom didn't say anything. She just looked at Braden.

Braden said, "I'll try very hard to get a job. Then I can make some money. And I can pay Dad back. Will you get Dad to help me?"

His mom didn't look pleased with Braden. She said, "You heard what your dad said, Braden. You have to get a job first. And you have to make some money. Then talk to your dad about helping you get a car."

"But, Mom," Braden said.

"You heard what I said, Braden. You have to get a job first. So do that. And forget about buying a car right now," his mom said.

His mom wouldn't try to talk his dad into helping him. Braden was sure about that. So he could stop trying to get her to do that. It would be a waste of his time. And his mom might get mad at him too.

Braden said, "I've never tried to get a job before. So what should I do first, Mom?"

"Look at the help wanted ads in the paper first. Maybe you can find a job in there," his mom said.

"Good idea, Mom," Braden said.

Why didn't he think of that?

His mom said, "And you can walk downtown. Look in the store windows. Sometimes stores have help wanted signs in their windows."

Braden went back into the den. He got the paper off of the table. He read the help wanted ads. And he found some places to go to look for a job.

Braden put the paper back on the table. Then he went into the kitchen. He said, "I'm going downtown to look for a job, Mom. I'll be back in time for lunch."

"Okay, Braden. Good luck," his mom said.

Braden hurried out of the house. And he started to walk downtown. He walked for a while.

Then he saw the car dealer that had the used car he wanted. He wanted to see the car. So he walked onto the lot. And he started to look for the car.

A man hurried over to Braden. The man worked there. He said, "I'm Mr.

Perez. Can I help you, young man?"

"I saw an ad in the paper about a car for sale here. And I want to look at it," Braden said.

"Which car is it? I'll be glad to show it to you," Mr. Perez said.

Braden told Mr. Perez which car he wanted to see. And Mr. Perez took him over to the car.

Braden looked at the car for a few minutes. He'd been right. It was just what he wanted.

Mr. Perez said, "What do you think, young man? This is a really great car. At a really great price. Do you want to buy it?"

"I sure do. But I don't have any money. My dad said he would help me get a car. But he said I have to get a job first. And earn some money. Then he'll help me," Braden said.

"Do you have a job?" Mr. Perez asked. Braden said, "Not yet. But I'll look for a job as soon as I leave here."

"It's too bad you don't have a job now. This is a really great car. At a really great price," Mr. Perez said again.
And Braden thought that too.

"I'm sure I'll be able to sell this car very soon. So you'd better find a job right away. Or this car will be gone," Mr. Perez said.

Braden thought it would be gone soon too.

He had to get a job. And he had to get one right away. But where could he find one?

chapter 3

It was the same morning. Braden had been to three stores to ask about a job. And he hadn't found one. But he'd seen some boys from his high school. And they were looking for summer jobs too.

Braden was walking down the sidewalk. He was thinking about where he should go next. He thought he might go to the tire store. Maybe he'd have better luck there.

A girl walked out of a store. And Braden almost bumped into her. She'd been in some of Braden's classes at school. Her name was Ruby.

"Hi, Braden. Why are you downtown?" asked Ruby.

Braden said, "I'm looking for a summer job. Why are you down here?"

"The same reason. To find a job. Have you found one?" Ruby asked.

Braden said, "No. How about you?"

"Not yet. But I won't give up. I'll keep looking. And I need to look some more now. So I can't stay and talk. Good luck on finding a job, Braden," Ruby said.

"Good luck to you too, Ruby," Braden said.

Ruby hurried down the sidewalk. And Braden started to walk to the tire store.

A boy called to him. "Braden, where are you going?" the boy asked.

Braden stopped. And he turned around to see who'd called to him.

It was his friend Kwame. Kwame had been in some of his classes too.

Braden said, "Hi, Kwame. Why are you downtown?"

"I'm looking for a job. But I haven't had any luck yet. What about you? Why are you down here?" Kwame asked.

"I'm looking for a job too. And I haven't had any luck," Braden said.

"Where are you going now?" Kwame asked.

"I thought I might go to the tire store," Braden said.

"I'll go with you. Is that okay with you?" Kwame asked.

"Yeah, it's fine with me," Braden said. He hadn't had any luck so far. And maybe Kwame would bring him some luck.

The two boys walked to the tire store. And they went into the store.

A man said, "Can I help you two boys

find some tires?"

"We don't need any tires," Braden said.

"What are you looking for?" the man asked.

"A job. Do you have a summer job?" Braden asked.

"Sorry, we don't need any extra help right now. But I hope you can find a job somewhere else," the man said.

"Thanks," Braden said.

"Yeah, thanks," Kwame said.

Then the two boys walked to the door. And they went outside.

Kwame said, "Too bad you didn't get a job there."

"Yeah, I need one. And I need one right away," Braden said.

"Why? I want a job for some extra money. But you sound like you need one for some other reason," Kwame said.

"I saw a car I want to buy. My dad

said he would help me buy it. But first I have to find a job. And earn some money," Braden said.

"You do need a job. And you need one right away. I just hope we can both find one," Kwame said.

"So do I," Braden said.

"What are you going to do now?" Kwame asked.

Braden said, "I don't know. I'm tired of looking for a job. I've been looking all morning."

Kwame said, "I think I'll go to the hardware store next. Do you want to go with me?"

"Sure, why not?" Braden said.

Braden wasn't having any luck. So he might as well go along with Kwame. And maybe they would both be lucky. And maybe they'd both find a job there.

chapter

4

The two boys walked down the side-walk. They came to the hardware store. And they stopped walking.

Kwame said, "I sure hope I can find a job here."

"I hope you can too," Braden said. He hoped they both could find a job there.

Kwame pushed open the door to the hardware store. And he went into the store. Braden went in right behind him.

Kwame walked over to a man. The man was behind a counter.

Kwame said, "Are you the owner?"

"I sure am. My name is Mr. Duvall. What can I do for you?" the man asked.

Kwame had a big smile on his face. He said, "My name is Kwame. I need a summer job. Are you hiring any teens just for the summer?"

Mr. Duvall said, "Sorry, but I can't help you, Kwame. I always need some-one to help me during the summer. But I just hired a boy this morning. And I don't need anyone else right now."

The smile left Kwame's face. He said, "I'm sorry to hear that. But I thought you would say that."

Braden had thought Mr. Duvall would say that too.

Mr. Duvall said, "I might need someone else in a week or two. Leave your phone number with me. And I'll call you if I do. Or if I hear about a job somewhere else."

"Thanks very much," Kwame said.

Kwame quickly wrote his cell phone number on a piece of paper. And he gave the paper to Mr. Duvall.

Mr. Duvall said, "I might not have a job for you later. So keep looking for a job. But I'll be sure to call you if I need you."

"Thanks. I hope you need me soon. But I'll keep looking for a job," Kwame said.

Kwame started to the door. Braden was right behind him. The two boys walked out of the store. And they started to walk down the sidewalk.

Kwame said, "Do you think Mr. Duvall will call me?"

"I don't know," Braden said.

"I hope he does. Mr. Duvall was very nice. And I'd like to work for him," Kwame said.

"He told you to keep looking for a job. So you'd better do that," Braden said.

Kwame said, "Yeah, I will. One thing's for sure. I need to get a job somewhere."

"So do I," Braden said.

But Braden didn't know where he would find one. Too many kids were looking for summer jobs. And he didn't think there would be enough jobs for all of them.

chapter 5

It was three days later. Braden was at home. He was in the den. He was watching a show on TV.

He had looked for a job for most of the day. And now he was tired. And he didn't think he would ever find a job.

His mom called to him. She was in the kitchen. She said, "Braden, I need you to go to the grocery store. I need a few things before I can cook dinner."

Braden turned off the TV. And he hurried into the kitchen.

Braden said, "What do you need at the store, Mom?"

His mom told him what she needed at the store. Then she said, "You won't forget what I said I wanted. Will you?"

"No, Mom. I won't forget," Braden said.

"Maybe I should write it down for you," his mom said.

Braden said, "You don't have to do that. I won't forget."

His mom quickly got a pen and some paper. She wrote down what she wanted at the store. Then she gave the paper to Braden. And she gave him some money.

She said, "I don't think you'll need all of this money. So be sure you bring the change back to me."

"I will," Braden said.

"And hurry back. It isn't too long until I have to start dinner," his mom said.

"Okay, Mom. I'll be back soon," Braden said.

Braden hurried out of the house. And he started to walk quickly to the store.

The store was only four blocks from his house. So it wasn't long until Braden got to the store. Braden hurried inside.

He got a cart. And he started to push the cart through the store. He quickly got what his mom wanted. Then he got in one of the checkout lines.

A man got in line behind him. Braden knew the man. The man was Mr. Duvall.

Mr. Duvall said, "Hi, aren't you the boy who came in my store the other day? The one who was with Kwame?"

"Yes, I am," Braden said.

"I'm glad I saw you. I want to call your friend Kwame. But I put his phone number somewhere. And now I can't find it," Mr. Duvall said.

Why did Mr. Duvall want to call Kwame? Did he have a job for Kwame?

Mr. Duvall said, "Is your friend still looking for a job?"

"He might be. But I don't know for sure. I haven't talked to him today," Braden said.

"I told Kwame I would let him know if I had a job. Can you give him a message for me?" Mr. Duvall asked.

"Sure," Braden said.

Mr. Duvall said, "Tell Kwame I have a job for him. The boy I hired quit. He said the job wasn't any fun."

Braden didn't care if a job was fun. He just wanted a job.

Mr. Duvall said, "Tell Kwame I need someone to unpack boxes. And to put things on shelves and tables for me. The job will last all summer. And I'd like for Kwame to start tomorrow."

Braden wished the job was for him. And not for Kwame.

Mr. Duvall said, "Tell Kwame to call me tomorrow morning. Or he can come by my store. Then he can let me know if he wants the job. Can you tell him that for me?"

"Sure," Braden said.

"Thanks," Mr. Duvall said.

Braden said, "Do you have more than one job? Or is it only one job?"

"Only one. And be sure to tell your friend Kwame," Mr. Duvall said.

"I will," Braden said.

Braden wanted the job. And he needed the job. So maybe he shouldn't tell Kwame about the job. Maybe he should try to get the job for himself. And hope that Kwame never found out what he did.

chapter

6

It was the next morning. Braden was on his way to the hardware store. He'd thought about the job all night. And he'd thought about how much he wanted the car. And he knew he needed the job. So he could buy the car.

Braden got to the hardware store. He went into the store. And he walked quickly over to Mr. Duvall.

Braden had made up his mind about what he'd do. He would lie to Mr. Duvall. And he wanted to talk to Mr. Duvall as soon as he could. Before he changed his mind about lying.

Mr. Duvall said, "Hi, I'm glad you came by this morning. Did you get a chance to talk to Kwame?"

"I sure did," Braden said.

But that was a lie. And Braden hoped his face didn't show that he was lying.

Mr. Duvall said, "Did you tell Kwame I have a job for him?"

"I sure did," Braden said.

"Did you tell Kwame to call me about the job? Or to come by here today? And did you tell him he could start today?" Mr. Duvall asked.

"Yes, I did," Braden said.
But none of that was true.

Mr. Duvall said, "I thought Kwame would be here by now. Or he'd have called by now. Does he want the job?"

"No, Kwame said he found a job.

And he said he'd already started to work there," Braden said.

Mr. Duvall looked surprised by what Braden said. He said, "That surprises me. I didn't think Kwame would be able to find a job so soon. What kind of job did he get?"

Braden hadn't thought Mr. Duvall would ask him that. So for a few seconds he couldn't think of an answer. But then he said, "I don't know. Kwame didn't say. But he seems to like the job a lot."

And that was a big lie too.

Mr. Duvall said, "I'm glad to hear that. But I wish Kwame had waited. So he could work for me. I sure do need someone. And I need someone now."

Braden was glad Mr. Duvall said that. Braden needed the job. And that gave him a chance to say how much he needed it.

Braden said, "Kwame has a job now. So I guess it's okay to say this now. But I didn't want to say it when I was here with Kwame."

"What? Why didn't you want to tell me then?" Mr. Duvall asked.

"I was here with Kwame then. It was his idea to come here. And he was trying to get a job. So I didn't want to say I was looking for a job too," Braden said.

Mr. Duvall got a big smile on his face. He said, "You are? That's great. Would you like to work for me?"

"I sure would," Braden said.

"Glad to hear that. When can you start?" Mr. Duvall asked.

"Today if you want me to," Braden said.

"I sure do. You can start right now," Mr. Duvall said.

That's what Braden hoped Mr. Duvall would say.

Braden was glad to have a job. And he could hardly wait to start. But he knew Kwame should have had the job.

What Braden did was wrong. And he knew that. And he tried to keep from feeling bad about what he'd done. But he did feel bad.

chapter 7

It was that night. Braden was at home. He was eating dinner with his mom and dad.

His dad looked at Braden. He said, "Your mom said you found a job today."

"Yes, I did," Braden said.

But Braden didn't want to talk about it. He didn't want his dad to find out how he got the job.

His mom said, "How do you like your new job, Braden? Did you have a good first day?"

"Yes, I like what I do. And the pay's good," Braden said.

His dad said, "You were lucky to get that job, Braden."

But Braden knew he wasn't lucky. He got the job only because he lied.

"Maybe in a few days we should go to the car dealer, Braden. And see if that car you like is still there," his dad said.

"That would be great, Dad," Braden said. He hoped the car would still be there.

His dad said, "A lot of kids are looking for jobs this summer. And not all of them are finding jobs. So you sure were lucky to find that job, Braden."

"Yeah, I know," Braden said.

He hoped his dad never found out how he got the job. And he hoped his dad would quit saying he was lucky. He wasn't.

Braden quickly ate his dinner. He didn't want to talk any more about his job.

Then he went to his bedroom. And he closed the door.

Braden's cell phone rang about ten minutes later. He looked at the caller ID to see who it was.

It was Kwame.

Braden didn't want to talk to Kwame. But he knew he should answer. So he could find out what Kwame wanted. And if Kwame knew he was working for Mr. Duvall.

Braden answered the phone.

Kwame said, "Hi, Braden. It's Kwame. Have you had any luck finding a job?"

"No, not yet," Braden lied.

He didn't want to lie to Kwame. But he had to lie. And he was glad Kwame didn't know he was working for Mr. Duvall. And he didn't want Kwame to find that out.

Kwame said, "I'm having bad luck too. I've looked all day for the last four days. And nothing. I'm thinking I won't find a job this summer."

Braden didn't want to hear that. Kwame had to find a job.

"Don't say that, Kwame. And don't stop looking for a job. You'll find one," Braden said. But he wasn't sure Kwame would.

Kwame said, "I thought I would've heard from Mr. Duvall by now. I was hoping he would call me. And tell me he has a job for me. But I don't guess he's going to call me."

Braden didn't say anything.

"I think I might call him," Kwame said.

Braden didn't want Kwame to call Mr. Duvall. So Braden knew he should say something. But he didn't know what he should say.

Kwame said, "What do you think I should do, Braden? Do you think I should call Mr. Duvall?"

"No, don't do that," Braden said. He said it too quickly.

"Why did you say I shouldn't call Mr. Duvall?" Kwame asked. He sounded surprised.

"Mr. Duvall might think you're pushing him for a job. And you don't want Mr. Duvall to think that. Then he might not want to hire you," Braden said.

"I never thought of that. Thanks for telling me that. You're a good friend, Braden," Kwame said.

But Braden knew that wasn't true. He'd lied to Mr. Duvall. And now he'd lied to Kwame.

Braden felt bad that Kwame hadn't

found a job. And Braden knew Kwame might not be able to find a job. But Braden couldn't do anything about it now.

Braden couldn't tell Mr. Duvall and Kwame that he'd lied to them. He'd lose his job. And his chance to get the car. And his friend.

chapter

8

It was the next morning. Braden had just gotten to the hardware store.

Mr. Duvall said, "Good morning, Braden. I want to ask you something."

"What?" Braden asked. He hoped it wasn't about Kwame.

Mr. Duvall said, "I need one more person to help me this summer. Do you know someone who's looking for a summer job?"

"No, Mr. Duvall. I don't," Braden lied.

But that wasn't true. He knew Kwame

was still looking for a job. But he couldn't tell Mr. Duvall about Kwame. Or Mr. Duvall would know Braden had lied to him.

Braden wished he hadn't lied to Mr. Duvall. Now Mr. Duvall needed two people to work for him during the summer. And both he and Kwame could've worked for Mr. Duvall.

But it was too late for that now. He'd lied. And he had to stick to the lie that Kwame had a job.

The store phone rang.

Mr. Duvall said, "Think about what I said, Braden. And maybe you'll think of someone who's looking for a job."

Then Mr. Duvall went to answer the phone.

A few minutes later, he came over to Braden. He looked very mad.

Braden hoped Mr. Duvall wasn't mad

at him. But Braden had a feeling he was.

Mr. Duvall said, "I just got a surprise, Braden. That was Kwame on the phone. He was calling to ask me about a job."

So Mr. Duvall knew Braden had lied. And that was why he looked so mad.

Mr. Duvall said, "Kwame said he doesn't have a job. And he said you know that. And he said you never gave him my message about a job."

Braden didn't say anything.

"So that means you lied to me, Braden. And you lied to your friend Kwame," Mr. Duvall said.

"I needed the job," Braden said.

"A lot of people need jobs, Braden. But they don't lie to get them," Mr. Duvall said.

Braden knew that was true. And Braden knew he didn't have to lie. But he'd lied.

Mr. Duvall said, "You lied to me to get this job, Braden. And I don't want you to work for me any longer. You can't be trusted. You might steal from me," Mr. Duvall said.

That surprised Braden very much. He couldn't believe Mr. Duvall thought he would steal.

"I would never steal from you, Mr. Duvall," Braden said.

"But how can I be sure about that, Braden? You stole the job from your friend Kwame," Mr. Duvall said.

"But that isn't the same thing. That was only a job. I would never steal money from anyone," Braden said.

"But that's sort of what you did. Isn't it, Braden?" Mr. Duvall said.

Braden didn't know what Mr. Duvall meant by that.

"I don't know what you're talking

about, Mr. Duvall. I didn't take money from anyone," Braden said.

"But you did, Braden. I would've paid Kwame for working for me. And you stole the job from him. So you were the one I would've paid. Not him. So you were also stealing the money from Kwame," Mr. Duvall said.

Braden had never thought about it that way. Braden said, "I never thought about it that way."

"Maybe you didn't, Braden. But I don't know that for sure. And I don't want you to work for me. I can't trust you," Mr. Duvall said.

Braden was sorry Mr. Duvall felt that way about him.

Mr. Duvall said, "I'll pay you for the time you worked, Braden. But I want you to leave."

Braden wished he'd never taken the

job away from Kwame. But he did. He double-crossed his friend. Both of them could've worked for Mr. Duvall. But now only Kwame would have a job.

Braden had lost his job. And his chance to get the car. And probably his friend. He wished he'd never lied to Mr. Duvall and Kwame.

consider this...

1. Why did Braden's dad want him to get a job?

2. Why didn't Braden's dad just loan him the money?

3. Was Braden a good friend to Kwame?

4. What should Braden have done differently?

5. How far would you go to get something that you desperately want?